CR

WOLFIE & FLY

WOLFIE & FLY

BAND ON THE RUN

Cary Fagan

WITH ILLUSTRATIONS BY Zoe Si

tundra

Tundra Books, an imprint of Penguin Random House Canada Young
Readers, a Penguin Random House Company

Library and Archives Canada Cataloguing in Publication
Fagan, Cary, author
Wolfie and Fly : band on the run / Cary Fagan ; illustrated by Zoe Si.
(Wolfie and Fly ; 2)
Issued in print and electronic formats.
ISBN 978-1-101-91823-4- (hardcover).—ISBN 978-1-101-91824-1
(EPUB)
I. Si, Zoe, illustrator II. Title. III. Title: Band on the run.
PS8561.A375W653 2018   jC813'.54   C2017-902658-5
                                                  C2017-902659-3

Published simultaneously in the United States of America by Tundra Books
of Northern New York, an imprint of Penguin Random House Canada
Young Readers, a Penguin Random House Company

Library of Congress Control Number: 2017939377

Edited by Samantha Swenson
Designed by Rachel Cooper
The artwork in this book was rendered in ink and watercolor.
The text was set in Fournier.

Printed and bound in the United States of America

www.penguinrandomhouse.ca

1   2   3   4   5   22 21 20 19 18

Penguin
Random House
tundra   TUNDRA BOOKS

To Marie Campbell
—Cary Fagan

For A & C, our little rock stars
—Zoe Si

CHAPTER I

Sleeping Wolf

"I just think it would be a nice thing," said Wolfie's mom.

"I do too," said Wolfie's dad. "The school talent show is a real tradition. Performing in it will get you out of your shell."

"I like being in my shell," said Wolfie.

"Besides, I don't know how to do anything, and the show is tonight."

It was Saturday morning. Wolfie was sitting at the kitchen table reading a book about helicopters. She found helicopters very interesting. They needed two rotor blades: a big one on

top to give it lift and a little one on the tail to prevent it from spinning around in a circle.

"That's right," said her mom. "You don't do anything. But you should. That's why we want you to go to the dance class at school this morning. You

might enjoy it. And then you can be part of the dance at the talent show."

"No, thank you." She turned the page.

"Just give it a try," pleaded her dad. "You don't take any extra classes. You've already dropped out of singing, pottery, karate, drama and yoga for kids."

Wolfie looked up. "I believe that is called a pattern, Dad. The pattern shows that I don't like taking classes."

"Well, it's a bad pattern," said her mom. "You're missing out on too much. And we've been too easy on you. So you're going to dance class this morning, and that's the end of the discussion."

Wolfie stood against the wall of the

school gymnasium. Ms. Stuckley, the gym teacher, was also the dance teacher. She asked everyone to warm up, and boys and girls began swooshing their arms through the air or spinning in circles or skipping across the floor.

The boys wore gym shorts. The girls wore leotards. Some had on frilly tutus. Most of them were pink. Wolfie hated pink. She was wearing her usual outfit— a white T-shirt, overalls and sneakers.

Ms. Stuckley clapped her hands. "All right, everyone, listen up. This is the last rehearsal before the talent show this evening. But if you haven't come to class before, you can still be in the chorus. The steps are easy."

Just then the gym door flew open and

a boy tumbled through. He got up and smiled. Oh no, thought Wolfie, it's Livingston Flott!

Livingston was Wolfie's next-door neighbor. He always called her Wolfie, although her real name was Renata Wolfman. And he wanted her to call him Fly.

Fly was such a nuisance. He always wanted to come over to play. He couldn't understand that Wolfie wasn't interested in playing with other kids. She liked being alone and didn't want any friends. Besides, playing was for babies. Wolfie was interested in grown-up things like science. Sure, there was that one time when Fly came over and they had built a submarine together and strange things had happened. But she had managed to avoid him ever since.

"Hi, Ms. Stuckley," Fly said. "Sorry I'm late. That sure is a nice hairstyle you have today. Did I miss anything?"

"Not to worry. We're just about to start our last warm-up exercise before the rehearsal. Listen up, everyone. I want each of you to think of an animal that you would like to be. And when I clap my hands, I want you to move around the room like your animal. Does everyone have an animal in mind?"

"I do, I do!" cried Fly. All the other kids nodded their heads. Ms. Stuckley clapped her hands.

A girl got down on all fours and stretched her back like a cat.

A boy began to hop like a bunny.
Another girl galloped like a horse.

Fly began to zip around the room,
flapping his wings and buzzing. It
wasn't hard to figure out what he was.

And Wolfie? She pondered a moment
and then lay down on the gym floor and
stayed still.

Ms. Stuckley came over and looked down at her. "What sort of animal are you?" she asked.

"I'm a wolf."

"Really?" said Ms. Stuckley. "But you're not moving."

"I'm a *sleeping* wolf."

"Will you be getting up soon?"

"Wolves can sleep for ten hours," said Wolfie.

CHAPTER 2

A Little Favor

"Seriously?" said Wolfie's mom when they got home again. "Lying on the floor for half an hour? Without moving?"

"It really wasn't funny, Miss Smarty-Pants," said her dad.

"Pants can't be smart. And I wasn't trying to be funny."

Her parents looked at each other. "Okay," said her mom. "Maybe dance isn't for you. But I still think it would be good for you to be in the talent show. You don't participate enough."

"To participate or not to participate, that is the question," said Wolfie, looking at her book on helicopters. There was a fascinating picture of a helicopter cockpit. The pilot had to be well trained and alert at every moment. She tried to imagine that the kitchen chair was a helicopter pilot's seat. She would have one control lever on her left side and another between her knees for her right hand to operate. Also a pedal for each foot.

"I'll make you a grilled cheese

sandwich," said her dad. "And then we're all going to Uncle Bob's house."

"What for?"

"Because he's having an art show," said her mom. "After your uncle retired from his job at the Perfecto Toaster Company, he got bored. So he started painting pictures."

"What does he paint pictures of?" Wolfie asked.

"Toasters," said her dad.

"That does sound thrilling," Wolfie said. "But I'd rather stay home. I've got an idea. You let me stay and I'll spend at least five minutes trying to come up with something for the talent show."

"How about ten minutes?" said her mom.

"Deal."

Wolfie ate her sandwich, careful to leave the crusts. Then she waited for her parents to go to Uncle Bob's. She couldn't understand why adults took so long to go anywhere. They were always deciding at the last minute to change their shirts or shoes, or else they couldn't find their wallets or keys. But at last her parents went to the front door.

"Don't touch the stove!" said her mom. "Don't let in any strangers. We miss you already!"

They closed the door. Hurray! At last Wolfie had the house to herself. There was nothing she liked better than being alone. Now she could read her book in peace.

Ding-dong!

Who could be at the door? She decided to ignore it.

Ding-dong, ding-dong, ding-dong, ding-dong . . .

"Stop ringing the bell!" she shouted through the door. "Who is it?"

"It's Livingston Flott!" came the answer. "Your friend! Fly!"

"You're not my friend."

"Oh, right. But let me in anyway."

"I'm not allowed to let in strangers."

"But I'm not a stranger!"

"No, but you *are* strange."

"Let me in. Pretty please?"

"Go away, Fly!"

Wolfie held her breath. But the doorbell didn't ring again. Fly didn't call out. Had he really gone home? Maybe she would get some peace and quiet after all.

She heard a clattering sound.

Wolfie turned around just in time to see Fly climbing in through the open living room window. On his back he had his plastic guitar. He got his other foot over the windowsill and fell onto the floor.

"Whoa! That last step is a doozy."

"You weren't invited in," Wolfie said.

"Your mom told me I could come over any time." Fly brushed himself off. "Besides, I need your help."

"For what?"

"For the school talent show."

"I thought you were going to be in the dance performance."

"Nah. I couldn't get the steps. Ms. Stuckley said it didn't matter, I could do my own steps or I could be a tree. But then I thought that I should do what I'm really good at. You know what that is."

"Talking?" said Wolfie. "Inviting yourself in? Falling through open windows?"

"No. Making up songs! You've heard me do it already."

"I've definitely heard you. But if you're going to sing at the talent show, you don't need me."

"I need your advice. You see, I have

this new song I just wrote. And it's a super-duper song. Maybe one of the greatest songs of all time. But when I sing it, something's not right. I can't figure out what it is. So I want you to listen and tell me."

Wolfie scratched her head. "And that's all you want?"

"Yup."

"All right. If it doesn't take too long." She sat down on the arm of the sofa. "Go ahead and sing."

CHAPTER 3

Clang Thump Ting Thump

Fly stepped into the center of the room. He moved his plastic guitar from back to front. He plucked the four strings to see if they were in tune. He cleared his throat.

"Well?" said Wolfie.

"You can't rush an artist." He straightened up, strummed his guitar and began to sing.

This is my song; it isn't yours.
I've made it up; my mom adores—
                              It!

Here is the tune; here are the words.
My brother thinks it's for the birds—
                              Blah!

It'll make me cool, this song of mine
Because it proves I'm good at rhyme—
                              See?

And now I'm out of things to say,
So I'll sing my song in the exact same way
                              Again!

Fly started at the beginning and sang all the verses again. Then he started it a third time.

"Hold on a second," Wolfie interrupted him.

Fly stopped. "What is it?" said Fly. "Did you find the problem?"

"I think a song that goes on and on

forever is a bit of a problem."

Fly snapped his fingers, or tried to. "You're right! I need one final verse. Let me think a minute."

He paced back and forth, muttering words under his breath. He stopped and stared up at the ceiling.

"What are you doing?"

"I'm looking for inspiration. Wait, I've got it! Here, listen to this."

He strummed the guitar again.

But every song does need an end,
And the rules of songs I will not bend—
The end!

He hit the guitar one last time and stood there expectantly. "Well?"

"That definitely is an ending," said Wolfie. "In fact, it uses the word *end* twice."

"Now I'm ready for the talent show. And I bet I'm going to win first prize too."

"There is one little problem still," Wolfie said.

"Really? Lay it on me."

"It's your timing."

"My timing?"

"It's off. Sometimes you speed up and sometimes you slow down. You need a steady beat."

"Hmm, a steady beat. Right. Good advice. Excellent, in fact. There's only one problem. I'm not very good at keeping a steady beat. Can you help me?"

Wolfie twitched her nose. She didn't want all her free time to get used up helping Fly. On the other hand, it was a challenge to figure out a way to help him. And she liked challenges.

"Maybe I can show you," she said. She looked around, but there was nothing useful in the living room so she went into the kitchen. Fly followed her. She saw a plastic garbage can, took out the bag and turned it upside down. Then she got a couple of wooden spoons from the drawer. She sat on the floor.

"I'll tap out a steady beat. Listen. One two three four, one two three four . . ."

She held the spoons like drumsticks and hit the overturned garbage can with one and then the other. *Thump thump*

thump thump. Fly listened, bobbing his
head with each thump. He swung his
guitar around and began to strum in
time with Wolfie.

"That's it," she said. "Just keep the
same steady beat."

Fly strummed along, smiling. And
then suddenly he stopped.

"What's wrong?"

"Nothing. But you need something else." He went over to the counter and picked up a small metal pot. He turned the pot over and put it down next to the garbage can.

"Try hitting the pot every once in a while."

"Why?"

"Just try it."

She shrugged. "Okay."

Thump thump thump clang, thump thump thump clang . . .

Fly strummed his guitar again. The drumming and the guitar sounded good together.

Fly stopped again.

"Now what?" asked Wolfie.

"You need one more thing." He went

to the cupboard and opened the door.
He found a pot lid and took it out. Then
he took the paper-towel roll off its
upright stand. He put the stand on the
other side of the garbage can and
balanced the lid on it.

"There! A cymbal," he said. "Try
hitting this once in a while, too."

"Interesting," said Wolfie. And she
started again.

*Clang thump ting thump, clang thump
ting thump* . . .

"That's it!" Fly cried. He started to
strum, and then he began to sing.

This is my song; it isn't yours . . .

They went through the verses twice

before Fly sang the new ending. On the last word, Wolfie gave the cymbal and the garbage can a final crash.

"Yes!" shouted Fly, pumping his fist in the air. "That's it! That's the music I want! Guitar and drums. We rock! We're a band, Wolfie, we're really a band!"

CHAPTER 4

Pointy Hats

But Wolfie just grimaced at Fly. "I'm
not in a band," she said. "I was just
helping you get the beat."

"But don't you hear how good we
sound? You *have* to be in the band. It's
destiny! You have to play the talent
show with me for sure. We'll win first

29

place, I know we will."

Wolfie was about to tell Fly that she was not going to play in the talent show. But she hesitated. Didn't her mom and dad want her to be in the show? Maybe if she played with Fly, they would stop bugging her about taking after-school classes.

"Okay, I'll do it," she said.

"I knew you were going to refuse. But it might be the most important thing we've ever done together."

"I said that I would do it."

"Why do you always have to . . . Wait. Did you say you'll do it?"

"Uh-huh."

Fly jumped up and down. "Fantastic! Amazing! We're a band! This is so cool,

Wolfie. We're going to be a big hit.
Now we just need a name. How about
the Super Sounds?"

"That's awful."

"The Warthogs?"

"Even worse."

"Bugspray? The Bad Smells?
Strawberry Ice Cream?"

"Those are all terrible names. Why can't we just be Wolfie and Fly?"

"Hmm, let me think about that. How about Fly and Wolfie? Nah, it doesn't sound as good. Okay, we'll be Wolfie and Fly. There's just one more thing we need."

"What's that?"

"Costumes," Fly said. "We can't just sound good. We also have to *look* good. We need our own style."

Wolfie didn't like dressing up, not even for Halloween. She looked down at her overalls. "I like what I'm wearing."

"Oh sure, that's your look. But I should match it. And we can add some extras. Have you got rubber boots?"

"Of course. I wear them when it rains. Rubber boots are highly practical."

"Good. So we can both wear rubber boots. How about hats? I have two matching hats at home. Hold on, I'll go and get them. And my rubber boots too!"

Fly moved fast. He was probably afraid that Wolfie would change her mind and lock the door. And Wolfie did think about it. Did she really want to lose her whole Saturday?

But Wolfie didn't lock the door. Instead, she went to the mudroom and found her rubber boots. She wondered to herself why she was being so cooperative. Did she like having company? Did she want to be in the talent show? She had to admit that drumming was fun. She just didn't want to admit it to Fly.

She clomped back into the living room in her boots. Fly must have been sure that Wolfie would lock the door because he climbed back in through the window. His yellow rubber boots came through first and the rest of him followed.

He was wearing a white T-shirt and overalls, just like Wolfie.

"You've got your boots on!" he said in surprise. "Great! Here are the hats."

Fly held them out. Wolfie frowned. The hats were made of felt. One was blue and the other green, and they were both covered in polka dots.

They were also pointy.

"Aren't those clown hats?" she asked.

"Yup. Great, aren't they? Here, put the green one on."

Wolfie didn't see any point in arguing now, even if they were going to look ridiculous. She put on the hat. Well, if there was one thing that Wolfie didn't care about, it was how she looked to other people.

Fly made her stand beside him in front of the full-length mirror in the hall. There they were in their rubber boots and pointy clown hats.

"That's what I'm talking about," said Fly. "Nobody else is going to look like us."

"That's for sure," Wolfie agreed. "You know, the talent show isn't until this evening. Maybe you could go home for a while."

"Are you kidding? We've got to practice. Better yet, we've got to practice in front of an audience."

"But we don't have an audience."

"Wolfie, Wolfie, when are you going to start using your imagination?"

"I'm not sure that I have one."

CHAPTER 5

Stuffing

"All we have to do is make a pretend audience," said Fly. "What if we used our stuffies? You do have some stuffed animals, right?"

Wolfie hesitated. She didn't understand this love for stuffed animals that other kids had. She saw kids talk to their stuffed animals, and play with them, and cuddle them. Stuffed animals were just material and stuffing! They weren't real.

But she did have one stuffed animal. Uncle Bob had given it to her when she was little. It was a rabbit that Uncle Bob had named Fluffy because of its soft fur. And then one day, Wolfie had decided to put Fluffy in the bathtub to see if it would float. Fluffy did float, but after that its fur was never fluffy again.

She went to her room and found Fluffy under the bed. She came back to the living room and showed it to Fly.

"That's it? Just one?"

"How many do we need?"

Fly shook his head. "I have lots of

them. We need a big audience. I'll go get them."

And Fly was off again. Wolfie tried to shout that he could just use the door. But Fly didn't hear. A few minutes later, a stuffed zebra came flying through the window. Then a bear, a snake, a lion, a

turtle, a dog, a monkey, another bear
and a lot more. Last through the
window came Fly, polka-dot hat first.

"Okay," he said, straightening his
pointed hat. "Let's arrange the stuffies
on the sofa. You can help."

Wolfie picked up a zebra and dropped
it on the sofa. "No, not like that," Fly
said. He picked up the zebra and made it
look as if it were sitting. Then he put a
cat behind it. "We can have two rows,"
he said.

Together they lined up the animals.
They stepped back to take a look.

"Not bad," said Fly.

"But where is the stage?" Wolfie
asked.

"Right here in front."

"Don't we need a spotlight?"

"Hey, good idea!" Fly said. "You're getting the hang of it. We can use that standing lamp. Just aim the light in front of the animals."

"And we can close the curtains so the rest of the room is dark."

"Wolfie," said Fly. "You are

impressing me. Turn off the light. Okay, let's set up your drums. Then we can go outside the living room, and after our name is announced, we can rush onto the stage."

"I guess you are the announcer too," said Wolfie.

"Naturally."

Wolfie put the drums in front of the animals, arranging the garbage can, the pot and the cymbal. She kept the wooden spoons in her hand. Then they both went out of the room.

"Now," said Fly, "here is the important thing. We have to really believe that we're about to step onto a big stage. We have to believe that rows and rows of people are waiting to see us play."

"How do I do that?" asked Wolfie.

Fly started to say something but stopped. He thought a minute and then shook his head. "I don't know! You just have to try. Are you ready?"

"No," said Wolfie.

"Here we go!"

CHAPTER 6

Ladies and Gentlemen . . .

Wolfie stood just behind Fly in the darkened doorway. She tried to make herself believe she was about to step onto a real stage in a real theater. But how could you imagine what wasn't real? She closed her eyes.

"Ladies and gentlemen," said a

booming voice, "give it up for your favorite band, Wolfie and Fly!"

How strange, thought Wolfie. The voice didn't sound like Fly at all. She could tell he was stepping through the doorway, so she opened her eyes a little to follow.

She heard clapping.

She heard cheering.

She heard people chanting their names.

"*Wolfie and Fly, Wolfie and Fly . . .*"

Wolfie bumped into Fly. She opened her eyes all the way so she could get to her drums.

"Look!" cried Fly. "It's a full house!"

Wolfie looked. And saw that she was on a big stage with colored spotlights shining down on them. And out front were rows and rows of . . . people? Yes, hundreds of them, all cheering for her and Fly. How could that be? Where were the stuffed animals? Where was her living room?

Fly stepped up to a microphone on a stand. "Hello, fans!" he shouted. The

crowd roared louder. "It's great to see you all. And now we're going to play our latest single. Are you ready, Wolfie?"

How could she be ready? But she nodded anyway. She saw that there was a stool behind her drums and sat down. But what had happened to her drums? Where were the garbage can, the pot

and the pot-lid cymbal? Here instead was a *real* drum kit, with a big bass drum and two smaller drums on stands and three real cymbals.

She looked over at Fly. He wasn't holding his little plastic guitar anymore. He had an electric guitar plugged into a huge amplifier! But he didn't look confused. He was acting as if all this was perfectly normal.

"Okay, Wolfie," he cried. "Hit it!"

What else could Wolfie do? She raised her wooden spoons—only they had become real drumsticks—and she banged them together, one two three four! Then she hit the drums while Fly stroked a big power chord on the guitar and leaned toward the microphone.

This is my song; it isn't yours.
I've made it up; my mom adores—

> *It!*

Wolfie kept up the beat, stepping on the bass drum pedal, banging the smaller drums, making quick hits on the cymbals. Fly sang the next verses.

Here is the tune; here are the words.
My brother thinks it's for the birds—

> *Blah!*

It'll make me cool, this song of mine
Because it proves I'm good at rhyme—

> *See?*

The people in the crowd began to do the wave, standing up one after another and raising their arms in the air. Then they held up their cell phones to make hundreds of lights shining in the dark.

And now I'm out of things to say,
So I'll sing my song in the exact same way!

They started the song from the beginning again. But this time the audience sang along, their voices filling the concert hall. It was an amazing sound.

When the fourth verse was over, Fly shouted out, "Drum solo!"

Drum solo? Wolfie had never done a drum solo in her life. She hadn't even played drums until a half hour ago. But it seemed that when she was with Fly she could do things that she had never done before. So she took a breath and began to hit the small drums in double-time, every so often striking a cymbal or banging the bass drum. She moved from one drum to another, the sticks flying in her hands, and then came down on two cymbals with a tremendous crash.

People hooted and clapped and stamped their feet. Fly began the final verse.

But every song does need an end,
And the rules of songs I will not bend—
The end!

The electric guitar wailed one last time. Wolfie hit one last drum. The audience went wild. They cheered and whistled and waved their hands.

"We're a hit, Wolfie, we're a hit!" cried Fly.

"I guess we really are."

"Come on, we have to take a bow."

Fly urged her to stand up. And then they bowed together. "This is so great," said Fly. "It's too bad we don't have another song. We could do an encore."

At that moment a girl climbed onto the stage. She was older than them and had long hair and wore lipstick. She skipped toward Fly, bent down and kissed him on the cheek.

"Aw, gee." Fly blushed.

"Ugh," Wolfie said, making a face.

But the girl wasn't the only one to come up. Wolfie saw a boy climbing onto the stage, followed by another boy and a girl. And behind them more people pushed forward.

"Ah, Fly," said Wolfie.

"Yes?"

"Is it usual for the audience to start climbing onto the stage?"

They both stared. The crowd was moving quickly across the stage toward them. They were shouting, *"Wolfie and Fly! Wolfie and Fly! We love you! We want your autograph! Wolfie and Fly!"*

The people in front had almost reached them. "We're going to be trampled by our own fans!" said Fly. "We have to get out of here! Wait, grab the instruments!"

Grab the instruments? That was easy for Fly to say. He already had the electric guitar in his hands. But how could Wolfie pick up a whole drum set? She grabbed the two smaller drums and a cymbal.

Then they ran. Off the stage, past the back curtain and down a corridor. Wolfie could see a door marked *Exit*. She looked back. The fans were right behind them.

"Don't stop!" cried Fly. "Keep going!"

CHAPTER 7

Up, Up and Away

Wolfie and Fly ran out the exit. They reached the sidewalk and kept running. When Wolfie looked behind her, she didn't see anyone. "It looks like the coast is clear," she gasped.

"We better keep going," Fly said. They slowed down a little. Wolfie was afraid she might drop a drum. They went around a corner and stopped. A man was standing in front of a van with a microphone in one hand and a TV camera on his shoulder.

"There you are!" the man said. "I'm Kurt Kavetsky from FAB News. Would you mind if I interviewed you? After all, our viewers are huge fans of Wolfie and Fly."

"I don't see why not," Fly said. He licked his palm and then ran his hand through his hair.

Wolfie whispered, "Don't you think we should keep going?"

"Oh, Wolfie, you really don't understand anything about being in a famous band. It'll only take a few minutes."

"Excellent," said the man, holding out his microphone. Wolfie looked at him. Kurt Kavetsky looked strangely familiar. Why, he looked a little bit like her uncle Bob! Wolfie remembered the pirate they had encountered in their submarine adventure. He had looked like Uncle Bob too. But this reporter was bald and had a little mustache. Also, he talked in a high voice.

"So tell our viewers what it's like to be so famous," said the man.

"We're really just like ordinary people," said Fly. "Of course, we're super talented and have a million friends. And we're very, very rich. But otherwise we're just the same as everybody else."

"Fantastic!" said the man. "And where do you get the ideas for those amazing songs?"

"Well, Kurt," Fly went on. "It's hard to know where true inspiration comes from. It's a gift, really. I guess that's what makes us so special."

"And you, Wolfie," said the man. "Our viewers would love to know how you became such a great drummer."

"I don't know," Wolfie said.

"You're too modest," he said. "I have one last question. What kind of toast do you like?"

"Toast?"

"Oh, look! I see your fans have caught up with you."

Wolfie and Fly both turned to look. They saw the mob of fans coming up the road.

"*Wolfie and Fly! Wolfie and Fly! We love you! We want souvenirs! We want your shirt! We want your shoes! We want your pants!*"

"Run!" Fly cried. They went around the van and hurried down the street. The cymbal kept banging against Wolfie's knee as she ran. Ahead she could see a small green park.

"Let's go there!" she shouted. They ran toward it. But as she got closer, Wolfie saw something that made her jaw drop.

A helicopter.

It was sitting in the middle of the park. The big rotor blade went slowly around as the engine purred. As they got closer, she could see words painted on the side: *Wolfie and Fly.*

"I didn't know we had a helicopter," Fly said. "Cool! Let's get inside."

Wolfie looked behind her. The mob of fans was still coming. So she ran to the helicopter, opened the door, and threw the drums and cymbal into the back. She climbed in. The seat looked an awful lot like her kitchen chair at home.

Fly got in on the other side. "We better strap ourselves in. Do you know how to fly this thing?" He sounded a little nervous.

"Well, I read a book about it."

"That'll have to be good enough. You better get a move on. Look!"

Wolfie looked through the side window. The fans were almost on them! The engine was already running. She put her hand on the lever to her left. She put her other hand on the stick

between her knees. She placed her feet
on the pedals.

"Hold on," she said, gritting her teeth.

She pulled the lever. The main rotor
blade sped up, making a great whirring
sound. The helicopter shook as they
rose. They got about ten feet off the
ground. They tilted to one side and
then the other as she worked the
controls. When she looked out, she

could see the fans jumping up, trying to grab the underside of the helicopter.

"Can you get this thing to go any higher?" Fly asked.

Wolfie moved the levers. The helicopter rose up and forward, picking up speed. The whirring blades became so noisy they had to shout to be heard.

"Boy, that was close," Fly yelled.

Wolfie looked down and saw the houses and buildings and roads and playgrounds. "This is a very interesting view," she shouted. "You can see the layout of the town. It's like looking at a big map."

Fly said something, but the noise drowned him out.

"I can't hear you!" Wolfie yelled.

"I said, I wonder what that flashing

red light on the dashboard is."

Wolfie looked at the dashboard. There *was* a light flashing. The light was just above a dial. The needle on the dial pointed to the word *empty*.

"Fascinating," Wolfie shouted. "It looks like we're out of gas. Did you know that helicopters can't glide the way airplanes can? They don't have wings. They just go straight down."

"I don't like the sound of that," Fly yelled.

At that moment the engine sputtered and died. They could feel the vibrations from the rotor blade slowing down.

"This is not good," shouted Fly.

"You don't have to shout anymore," Wolfie said. "I can hear you fine."

The helicopter went down.

CHAPTER 8

The Show

Crash!
Thump!
Bang!

Wolfie felt herself thrown backward in her seat. She had her eyes shut tight. She was afraid to open them.

"Wolfie? Are you okay?"

She opened her eyes. For a moment she couldn't understand where she was, even though everything looked familiar. There were cupboards, a counter, a stove, a sink and a refrigerator. How strange, she thought. It looked like her own kitchen.

She was sitting in a chair, only the chair was tipped backward onto the floor. It wasn't a helicopter seat. It was her usual kitchen chair. And when she looked over, she saw Fly in the chair beside her. He had tipped backward too. But Fly's eyes were still closed.

"You can open your eyes," she said.

He blinked and looked around. Then he smiled. "We're in your kitchen! Cool."

Just then, Wolfie heard the front door open. "Oh, Renata!" called her mom. "Look what we have!"

Her mom and dad came into the kitchen. "What are you doing lying backward on the floor?" asked her dad.

"It's a really good view from here," said Fly.

"Look, Renata," said her mom. She held up a painting in a frame. The painting was of a toaster. The toaster had wings on it like a bird and was flying through the air.

"Did Uncle Bob paint that?" Wolfie asked.

"Yes, he did."

"Huh. Not as bad as I had expected." Wolfie got up from the floor, followed by Fly. As she pulled up her chair, she noticed her drums and cymbal behind her. Only they weren't the ones from the big stage. They were the garbage can, the pot and the lid.

"What time is it?" asked Fly.

"It's ten minutes to four," said Wolfie's dad.

"The talent show at school starts in ten minutes!" Fly cried, picking up his guitar. It had become a plastic guitar with four strings again.

"Are you going to be in the talent show? How nice," said her mom.

"Wolfie—I mean Renata—is going to be in it too," said Fly. "But we have to hurry."

"That's wonderful!" said her mom.

"I don't know why I agreed," Renata sulked. "I must have been feeling sorry for you."

"Feeling sorry for me?" said Fly. "Why, that's almost as good as liking me!"

"We better get going," said her dad. "We don't want to be late."

Together, the four of them hurried out of the house and down the sidewalk. It took only five minutes to get to school. The front entrance was lit up and a homemade sign hung above the door: *Talent Show Tonight!*

They went in. There was a boy a little younger than Wolfie sitting at a desk with a clipboard. Fly went up to him.

"We want to perform in the show. Please put our name down on the list."

"Here," said the boy, handing over the clipboard. "Write it down."

Fly picked up a pencil and wrote. He gave the clipboard back. The boy peered at the words.

"Wobber and Flish?"

"No, no! It says Wolfie and Fly."

"Your handwriting is very messy. Okay, you're the last act. You better get to the gym. They're about to start."

Through the doors of the gym they went. There was the gym teacher, Ms. Stuckley, standing at the front. A few rows of folding chairs had been set up. There were about twenty people sitting in the chairs.

"Hi, Mom! Hi, Dad!" said Fly to two people sitting at the front. "Wolfie, these are my parents, Georgina and Abner Flott. Mom, Dad, this is Wolfie and her parents."

Everyone said hello. Somehow she had expected Fly's parents to look strange. But they just looked like regular parents.

"Those costumes are just so adorable," said Mrs. Flott. Wolfie had forgotten that they were wearing identical rubber boots and overalls. Somehow they had managed to hold onto their pointy hats. Okay, Mr. and Mrs. Flott really were like regular parents.

"Let's get started," said Ms. Stuckley in a loud voice. "Would the contestants please sit in the front row? Thank you. Welcome, everyone, to the Hokum Street Public School talent show. Isn't this exciting? Let's plunge right in. First up is Arabella Snorr. It says here that Arabella is going to make the sound of a frog through her nose."

People clapped. Arabella came up. She put her hand against her nose and blew. She really did sound like a frog.

Pretty good, thought Wolfie.

Fly leaned over and whispered, "Ah, she's got nothing on us."

Next up was a boy named Tino Tisdale who recited a poem called "The Owl and the Pussycat" while balancing a glass of water on his head. He only spilled it on the last line. Pretty impressive, thought Wolfie.

Fly leaned over to whisper again, "He hasn't got a chance."

After him came Ms. Stuckley's dancers. The dancers sometimes bumped into each other. But they all managed to bow together at the end. Then Joyce Golden juggled three balls. She only dropped two of them.

Fly gave Wolfie the thumbs-up.

"And now," said Ms. Stuckley, looking at the clipboard, "we have one last performance. A singing duo. Please welcome Wobber and Flish!"

The two of them got up. Wolfie brought up her drum set.

"Renata!" called her mom. "You forgot these."

Her mom held out the two wooden spoons. But when Wolfie took them, she saw that they weren't spoons.

They were *real* drumsticks.

"Where did you get these?"

"They were on the kitchen floor."

This really was strange. Wolfie set up the garbage can, pot and cymbal. Not long ago she had seen two rows of stuffies somehow turn into a packed concert hall of screaming fans. Now the two of them were playing for a handful of parents and kids in the school gym.

"Hello, Hokum Street Public School!" shouted Fly. "Are you ready to rock?"

"I am," said a little girl, raising her hand.

"Good. We are going to play an original song. That means we made it up ourselves. Let's do it, Wolfie!"

Well, if she could play for a full house,

she could play for a handful of people in the school gymnasium. She banged the drumsticks together, *one two three four*. Fly began to strum his plastic guitar. It sounded out of tune but he didn't stop.

This is my song; it isn't yours . . .

They sang four verses and then Fly called for a drum solo. Wolfie started banging on the garbage can, the pot and the pot-lid cymbal. One of the drumsticks flew out of her hand. It flew up in the air and she just managed to catch it as it came down. Then they sang the final verse and stopped. A good thing, too, because just then one

of the strings on Fly's guitar broke with a loud *twang*.

The clapping sure didn't sound like it had in the concert hall. They went back to their seats.

"Well," said Ms. Stuckley, coming up front again. "Weren't all our student performers just wonderful? But now I am going to announce our talent contest winners."

"I should have written a speech," said Fly.

"Third prize," said Ms. Stuckley, "goes to . . . the Hokum Dancers. Well done! Second prize goes to . . . Arabella Snorr for her excellent frog sounds. And the first prize in this year's talent show goes to . . ."

Fly began to get up.

". . . Tino Tisdale for his poetry recital and impressive display of balance. Congratulations!"

"Hey," said Fly, "what do we get?"

"Oh, I'm sorry." Ms. Stuckley smiled at them. "I forgot to say that honorable mention goes to Wobber and Flish."

"Honorable mention!" said Fly. "Pretty sweet." He held up his hand to high-five Wolfie.

"What's that for?" Wolfie said.

"Never mind," said Fly.

CHAPTER 9

Celebration

Wolfie's parents hurried up to them,
followed by Fly's parents. "We're very
proud of both of you," said her dad.

"Yes, we are," said Fly's dad.
"Especially those adorable costumes.
And now we want to take you both out
for ice cream to celebrate."

"But we came in last," said Wolfie.

"You have to look on the positive side," said Fly. "We got an honorable mention. And now we get ice cream."

They all walked to the ice cream shop together. Wolfie ordered vanilla—it was the only flavor she liked. But Fly dithered over all the choices. "I can't decide if I should have raspberry caramel swirl or licorice chunky toffee."

He settled on peanut butter raisin. Their parents went to a table while Wolfie and Fly sat on the step outside. "That was some day," Fly said.

"I still don't understand what happened," said Wolfie.

"Some things just can't be explained. And now here we are, Wolfie and Fly, eating ice cream together. That's what I call a moment between friends."

"I never said we were friends."

"Okay, fine. But it sure is nice sitting here. You know what? I feel a song coming on."

"I was afraid of that."

"I don't have to sing it if you don't want me to."

"It's weird," said Wolfie, "but I actually *want* you to sing it. I'll see if you keep a steady beat without me."

"Sweet," said Fly with a grin as he gave Wolfie his ice cream to hold and picked up his guitar. "Very sweet."

ACKNOWLEDGEMENTS

Thanks again to ace editor Samantha Swenson and the crack team at Tundra Books. A finer bunch I never met.